# Danni
## the Drum
## Fairy

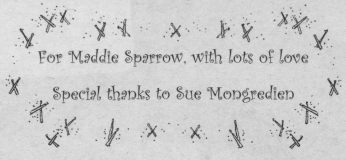

For Maddie Sparrow, with lots of love

Special thanks to Sue Mongredien

No part of this work may be reproduced, stored in a retrieval system, or transmitted in any form or by any means, electronic, mechanical, photocopying, recording, or otherwise, without written permission of the publisher. For information regarding permission, write to Rainbow Magic Limited c/o HIT Entertainment, 830 South Greenville Avenue, Allen, TX 75002-3320.

ISBN: 978-0-545-10627-6

12 11 10 9 8                                                        15/0

Printed in the U.S.A.

First Scholastic Printing, January 2010

# Danni
## the Drum
## Fairy

by Daisy Meadows

SCHOLASTIC INC.

New York   Toronto   London   Auckland
Sydney   Mexico City   New Delhi   Hong Kong

The
Fairyland
Palace

Ba

Wetherbury College

MALL

MEGA BIG NATURE

New Harmony Mall

The
Village
Hall

Willow Hill

The
Warehouse

I'm through with frost, ice, and snow.
To the human world I must go!
I'll form my cool Gobolicious Band.
Magical instruments will lend a hand.

With these instruments, I'll go far.
Frosty Jack, a superstar.
I'll steal music's harmony and its fun.
Watch out, world, I'll be number one!

# Contents

## Extra-Exciting

"Bye, girls. I'll see you later," said Mrs. Tate. "Have fun!"

"We will," Kirsty Tate replied, smiling. She leaned through the car window to kiss her mom good-bye. "Thanks for the ride. Bye!"

"Good-bye!" echoed Rachel Walker, Kirsty's best friend.

Both girls waved as Mrs. Tate drove away. Kirsty looked up at the warehouse building they were standing in front of, and grinned at Rachel. "What are we waiting for?" she said. "Let's get inside!"

Rachel's eyes were bright as she slipped an arm through Kirsty's. "I can't believe we're actually going to be in a music

video!" she said happily. "As if this vacation wasn't already fun enough!"

The two girls walked through tall glass double doors into the warehouse, feeling bubbly with anticipation. Rachel was staying with Kirsty's family for a week over school break, and on the very first day the girls had found themselves in another one of their wonderful fairy adventures. This time, they were helping the Music Fairies find their magic musical instruments, which had been stolen by Jack Frost and his goblins.

So far, the girls had helped the Music Fairies find three of the instruments, but there were still four missing. They had a lot of work to do!

Today, Kirsty and Rachel were in for a very different kind of adventure, though. Kirsty felt dizzy with excitement as she thought about it. She and Rachel were so lucky to be there. They were both big fans of Juanita, the pop star who'd rocketed to fame last year when she'd won the National Talent Competition. And now Juanita was making a video for her new song right in Wetherbury! Not only that, Mrs. Tate's friend, Mandy, had been hired as the makeup artist for the video shoot . . . and she'd asked Kirsty and Rachel if they'd like to appear in the video as extras! Both girls were so excited. They had been practicing the routine at home as much as possible.

Kirsty's and Rachel's legs were

trembling as they walked into the
warehouse. They found themselves in a
stylish lobby, with a reception desk plus
a couple of bright red sofas. A sign on the
far wall read VIDEO SHOOT THIS WAY, with
an arrow pointing along a long hall.

"That's us," Rachel said, nudging
Kirsty as she read the sign. There was a

friendly-looking woman behind the reception desk, who smiled at the girls as they approached. "Hi," Kirsty said. "We're here as extras for the video."

"Great," the woman said, passing a visitors' book to them. "If you could just sign in, I'll get someone to take you to the dressing rooms."

Kirsty and Rachel wrote down their names while the receptionist made a call.

Then a woman in a purple minidress stepped out of the hallway and smiled at them. "Hi, I'm Anna. Are you my extras?" she asked. "Come with me, girls, and I'll show you your outfits."

Anna led Rachel and Kirsty to the wardrobe area, chatting as they walked. "We're having a bit of a nightmare today, but it's nothing for you two to worry about," she said. "It's just that the instruments don't seem to be working properly. We wanted to practice for the shoot with the musicians actually playing, but we've had to tell them to just pretend, instead."

Kirsty and Rachel exchanged glances. They knew why the instruments weren't working — it was because some of the fairies' magic instruments were still missing! The Music Fairies made sure that all music in Fairyland and the human world was fun to play, and sounded harmonious. But when

the fairies didn't have their magical
instruments, music didn't sound as good.
In fact, it was all out of tune!

Jack Frost knew this — and he also
knew that whoever *did* have the
instruments would be able to make
fantastic music! The fairies had told
Kirsty and Rachel that this was why
he'd taken them in the first place. He'd
formed a band, and wanted to win next
week's National Talent Competition.
If Jack Frost's group, Frosty and his
Gobolicious Band, won, it wouldn't take
anyone long to figure out that Jack Frost
and the goblins weren't human. And
then, once the world discovered that
Fairyland existed, all of Kirsty's and
Rachel's fairy friends would be in terrible
danger from curious humans!

"Here we are!" said
Anna, opening a door
and leading the girls
into a room filled with
clothing racks. There
were all kinds of
colorful clothes and
accessories hanging
up, and shelves of

shoes, too.

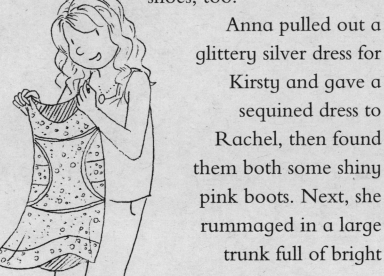

Anna pulled out a
glittery silver dress for
Kirsty and gave a
sequined dress to
Rachel, then found
them both some shiny
pink boots. Next, she
rummaged in a large
trunk full of bright

scarves and hats, and came up
with two pairs of headbands
with star-shaped
antennae for the girls
to wear. "Funky,
huh?" Anna
laughed. "The
song's called
'Cosmic Craze,' so
that's why
everyone's looking
all space-age."

The girls quickly
changed their
clothes, then Anna
took them to Mandy's
makeup room. It was
brightly lit, with a huge

mirror on one wall, and two
stools set up in front of it.
"Hello!" Mandy smiled.
"Take a seat, and I'll
turn you into little
alien girls."
Kirsty and Rachel
both sat down and
Mandy went to
work. She dabbed
some glitter in their
eyebrows and
painted silvery
swirls on their cheeks.
"Very cute," she
said. "Just a little sparkly
face powder, and you'll
be done."

She took out a silver tin of powder and
was about to lift the lid, when an anxious
man put his head around the door.
"Mandy? Could you touch up Juanita's
lipstick on set, please?"

"Sure," Mandy said at once. She
passed the silver tin to Kirsty. "Would
you mind dusting some of this over
each other's faces, please? I've
got to go."

She rushed out of the room and Kirsty lifted the lid off the tin. As she did, Danni the Drum Fairy burst out in a cloud of silver sparkles!

And ... Action!

"Oooh!" Kirsty said in surprise. Then she smiled at the little fairy. "Hello again," she said. She and Rachel had met all of the Music Fairies at the beginning of the week.

Danni had long blond hair swept off her face. She wore a short pink dress with

a wide silver hem and
neckline, as well as
black leggings and
sleek pink flats.

"Hi there," she said,
fluttering her wings to
shake off the sparkly face powder. She
gave a dainty sneeze as the powder
floated all around her. "I'm here to look
for my magic drums. I've got a feeling
they're somewhere nearby."

"Hi, Danni," Rachel said. "We'll help
you look for your drums!"

"Girls, you're wanted on the set!" came
another voice, and Mandy walked back
into the room. Danni had to make a
quick dive under Kirsty's ponytail so she
wouldn't be seen. Kirsty could feel the

little fairy's wings tickling the back of her neck as Mandy led her and Rachel to where the music video was being filmed.

There was a stage area at the back of a large room, where a guitarist, keyboard player, and drummer were positioned, with bright lights shining down on them. Glowing stars and planets dangled above their heads, and they all wore silver robot costumes. In the center of the stage was Juanita, wearing a shimmering turquoise

dress, her long black hair flowing down her back.

"Wow," Kirsty breathed, staring at the singer in awe. It was amazing to think that Kirsty and Rachel were going to be sharing a stage with such a famous person!

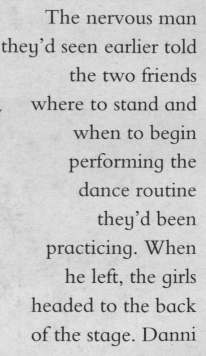

The nervous man they'd seen earlier told the two friends where to stand and when to begin performing the dance routine they'd been practicing. When he left, the girls headed to the back of the stage. Danni

peeked out from behind Kirsty's hair to
look at the drums that had been set up in
front of the drummer. "They're not
mine," she whispered in disappointment.

"And . . .
ACTION!"
called the
director. The
backing music
began, and
Kirsty and
Rachel started
dancing. They
couldn't help
noticing how
the drummer was
flailing around wildly
behind the drum set. He did not look
convincing at all.

"Cut!" the director shouted, striding over to the drummer. "What on earth are you doing?"

"I can't see out of this robot helmet," a muffled voice replied.

"Well, take it off then," the director ordered. "We'll get someone from the makeup team to paint your face alien-green instead."

Rachel nudged Kirsty as the drummer removed his helmet. She'd noticed that the drummer had very pointy ears. They looked suspiciously like a goblin's! The girls were finding it harder than usual to spot the goblins, because Jack Frost had cast a spell on them to take the green out of their skin. But there was no mistaking those pointy ears and nose!

"He's got big feet, too," Kirsty said, bending down to take a quick look. "He's definitely a goblin!" Mandy hurried on-stage and began dabbing bright green stage makeup all

over the goblin's skin. Kirsty and Rachel
had to struggle not to giggle at the
goblin's expression as his face changed
color. Jack Frost's spell didn't matter now!

"I don't know about 'alien-green,'"
Kirsty whispered. "It looks more like
goblin-green to me!"

Danni was smiling. "If a goblin is here, it means my magical drums are somewhere close by, too," she whispered excitedly. "Now all we need to do is find them!"

## Good-bye, Goblin!

"And . . . ACTION!" cried the director a few minutes later. The music started up again, but this time the girls heard a *second* drumbeat. Kirsty and Rachel stared at the goblin behind the drum set. They knew that all of the musicians were supposed to be pretending to play while the video was being filmed. They

should not be making any sound. But the girls could definitely hear the goblin's drumsticks hitting the cymbals and drums!

"He's taken off the muffle pads," Danni whispered. "No wonder we can hear what he's doing." Kirsty and Rachel could see some muffle pads on the ground, right where the goblin had thrown them.

"Cut!" came an impatient shout.

"Here comes the director again," Rachel murmured, "and he doesn't look very happy."

"Put those back on," the director snapped at the goblin. "We're never going to finish this video with you goofing around!"

The goblin scowled, but did as he was told.

"And . . . ACTION!" the director called a third time.

The goblin picked up his drumsticks and began playing again. Now that the

muffle pads were back on, there was almost no noise coming from the drums, but the girls could tell that the goblin was playing well and keeping perfect time. Danni began dancing to the rhythm on Kirsty's shoulder, and Rachel could see that she was tapping imaginary drumsticks in excitement.

"He's good," Danni whispered. "My drums *must* be very close by. I'm sure they're helping him play so well." Kirsty agreed. The magic musical instruments were full of such powerful magic that anyone who was near became

very talented at playing that particular
instrument. So the magic drums had
to be very close to the goblin — but
why couldn't the girls and Danni
see them?

Just then, a thought struck Kirsty.
"What if the magic drums are still at
their tiny Fairyland size?" she whispered
to Danni and Rachel. "The goblin might
have them hidden in his pocket!"

All three friends
stared at the
goblin, who was
now making up
a spectacular
drum solo that
didn't fit in with
the song or
video at all.

"CUT!" yelled the director. He sounded really angry now. "You're fired," he told the goblin. "Get off the set immediately! We'll use a different actor in your place."

The goblin put his nose in the air. "I'd rather rehearse with my own band anyway," he responded rudely and stormed off the set.

Rachel and Kirsty instinctively tried to follow him, but the director spotted them. "Girls — where are you going?" he called. "We need you here, please."

"Sorry," Kirsty said politely. As soon as the director had moved out of

earshot, she turned to Rachel in a panic. "What are we going to do? The goblin's getting away!"

"I'll follow the goblin so that we don't lose him," Danni suggested.

"But there are so many people around," Rachel reminded her. "We don't want anyone to see you!"

"We need to create a diversion," Kirsty suggested. "Something that will get everyone looking at us, so that Danni

can sneak away without anyone
noticing."

"What if I pretend to fall over and
bump into the drum set?" Rachel said.
"That'll make a lot of noise."

"Good idea," Danni said. "Let's try it."

Rachel scooted closer to the drums
and pretended to be practicing her dance
routine. Then she purposely stumbled and
knocked over the drums with a huge crash!

Just as the girls had hoped, everyone turned to look, and several people rushed over to help Rachel.

"Go!" Kirsty whispered, and Danni whizzed high into the air.

Out of the corner of her eye, Rachel caught sight of a tiny speck zooming out of the room. Danni had gone!

## Where's Danni?

A little while later, the director called for a break, and Rachel and Kirsty were told they could leave the set for half an hour. "Finally!" Kirsty said as she and Rachel ran out of the room in search of Danni and the goblin. "I'm dying to know what's been happening."

"I hope Danni's all right," Rachel said as they went along the corridor. "I've hardly been able to concentrate on dancing — I've been thinking about her the whole time!"

The girls were near a cafeteria now, and they looked in cautiously. There were chairs and tables set up where people were drinking coffee and eating sandwiches, but no sign of a goblin in a robot suit, or a tiny fairy. "Not there," Kirsty said. "Let's check in the dressing and makeup rooms."

The girls went down to the room with the clothes racks, then to Mandy's makeup room. Neither Danni nor the goblin were there, either. "I hope everything's all right," Rachel said anxiously. "Where could they be?"

"What's that?" Kirsty asked, crouching down to examine the floor. "Look, Rachel. Glitter!"

Rachel stared at the line of pink glitter along the ground. "I wonder if Danni's left us a glittery trail to follow?" she said, feeling excited.

"There's only one way to find out,"
Kirsty said, grabbing her friend's hand.
"Come on!"

The girls raced down the corridor,
following the glittery line. The trail led
to a small office on the far side of the
warehouse. They glanced around
the edge of the door, which was open,
and saw three goblins gathered around a
table. On top of the table was . . . a tiny
drum set!

"There it is," Rachel whispered,
her heart thumping.

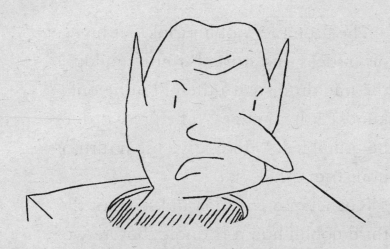

The green goblin who'd been in the video was glaring at the drum set. "Why didn't Jack Frost give us a wand to make this thing bigger and smaller when we need to?" he complained. "How am I supposed to practice for the band when my drums are so itsy-bitsy?"

"Grow!" another goblin ordered the drum set, pointing at it with a warty finger. "Grow, you silly thing!"

The drummer goblin took out his drumsticks and started trying to play the tiny drums with them, but he only knocked them over. "They're worthless," he grumbled. "Here, give me a turn on your triangle."

Rachel and Kirsty could see that the third goblin had a triangle that he was playing gently. At the very mention of sharing, he swung the instrument away. "No," he said protectively. "This is mine!"

Just then, Danni

appeared by the girls' shoulders. "Hi
there," she whispered. "I've been hoping
for a chance to fly in and grab my
drums, but the goblins never move far
enough away."

The three
friends racked
their brains
for what to
do next.

The goblins were still arguing about
playing the triangle. Their bickering
suddenly gave Rachel an idea. "Danni,
if you could conjure up some musical
instruments in a different room, we
might be able to lure the goblins out
of this one," she said. "Hopefully
they'll leave the magic drums here in
their excitement!"

Danni nodded, smiling. "I
could use my magic to
make some instruments,
but they won't last for
long," she said, "only
for a few hours.
Still — that
should be all
we need. Let's
try it!"

The three
friends headed
farther along the
hallway and found
an empty room just
next door. Once inside, Danni
waved her wand. Instantly, a selection of
instruments appeared in a neat line on the
floor — a tambourine, a xylophone, a

42

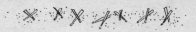

saxophone, a trumpet, and some
guitars and cymbals, all in
bright colors and sparkling
with fairy magic.
"They look great," Kirsty
said, picking up a pink
tambourine and giving it a
shake. "Very funky."
"Let's hope
the goblins are
tempted," Rachel
said. "Come on!"
They hurried
back to where the
goblins were still
arguing, and Danni
tucked herself under Rachel's hair.
If the goblins saw that a fairy was
around, they would be very suspicious!

"Good news," cried Kirsty as they entered the room. "We heard you saying you wanted to play some instruments, and I thought you'd like to know that there are lots next door."

"A trumpet, a saxophone, a tambourine . . ." Rachel listed. "And you can choose whichever ones you like!"

"Oooh," said the goblin with the triangle. "That sounds like fun."

"Yes," agreed the goblin who didn't have an instrument. "We can make lots of noise!"

Rachel held her breath as she waited for the drummer goblin to reply. He didn't look quite as tempted. "You two go," he told his friends. "I'm staying here to guard my drums."

"Why don't you just take a look?" Kirsty said persuasively. "They're really great instruments."

The goblin shook his head stubbornly. Rachel and Kirsty could only exchange helpless glances as they followed the other two goblins out of the room. The plan had failed. What else could they do to get Danni's drums back?

## A Small Surprise

"This way," Rachel told the two excited goblins, who were marching up and down the corridor like little children. She pushed open the door of the next room and both goblins rushed inside.

"Ooh, wow!" one squealed, racing over to the green trumpet and blowing into it.

"Look at me!" the second giggled, bashing away on the bright red xylophone.

"Choose whichever one you like," Kirsty said. She caught Rachel's eye. "We'll be back in the other room, OK?" The two friends rushed out, in a hurry to get back to the goblin with the magic drums. On the way, another idea popped into Kirsty's head. "Danni," she said curiously, "would you be able to make the goblin really small, so that he was the right size to play your drums?"

Danni fluttered
out from her
hiding place to
hover in front
of Kirsty's face.
"Sure," she
said. "Why?"

"Because then he
wouldn't be able to keep us from picking
up your drum set," Kirsty replied with a
smile.

"Good thinking!" Rachel said.

"Yes, that might work," Danni agreed.
"I like it, Kirsty!"

They went back into the first room,
where the drummer goblin was sitting
in front of the magic drums.

"Abracadabra!" he muttered.
"Hocus-pocus!"

"You're much too big for those drums," Kirsty told him.

"It's not me that's too big, it's these drums that are too small," the goblin grumbled in reply. "If only I could make them bigger . . . presto!" he cried, snapping his fingers hopefully. Nothing happened.

"Well," said Kirsty, "my friend here could use *her* magic to make them the right size for you. Then you'd be able to play them!"

The goblin looked at Danni suspiciously. He clearly didn't trust the fairy but seemed desperate to play the magic drums.

"All right," he said after a few

moments, expecting Danni to
make the drums bigger.
Danni grinned and waved
her wand . . . and the goblin
shrank to the size of a
matchstick!

At first,
the goblin
didn't seem to
realize what
had happened. He looked at the drum
set, saw that it was the right size for
him, and gave a yelp of delight. Then
he rushed over and began pounding
away with his drumsticks, which had
shrunk, too.

"Wow, he's good," Rachel said with admiration, as he beat out a fantastic drum roll.

Danni raised an eyebrow. "Only because my drums are magic," she reminded Rachel. "*They're* doing all the work, not him."

The goblin looked up at the sound of their voices — and did a double take when he saw that the girls now looked like giants! His mouth fell open as the truth hit him. "I've been tricked!" he wailed.

"That's right," Kirsty said cheerfully, reaching down to pick him up.

"Yikes!" he squealed. "Put me down!"

"I'll take these, thank you," Rachel said, scooping the magic drums into her palm.

The goblin, meanwhile, was kicking his tiny legs and shrieking, "Put me down!"

"I will," Kirsty promised, "just as soon as Danni has her drums back."

Danni soared toward Rachel, her

wings shimmering all the colors of the
rainbow as she flew. She was just
about to land on Rachel's palm when
the door flew open. In came the two
other goblins, carrying some of the

colorful instruments from the room
next door.

"HELP!" the tiny goblin squeaked to
his friends. "They're trying to steal the
magic drums!"

# Off to Goblin Grotto!

Danni tapped her wand on the snare drum in the nick of time. There was a flash of fairy magic, and then a pair of drumsticks appeared in Danni's hand. The magic drums flew up into the air with Danni, just as the goblins made a lunge for her. Their long fingers closed

around empty air as she darted out of reach.

"Give those back!" the tiny goblin shrieked, his little voice high-pitched and shrill. "I need them for Jack Frost's Gobolicious Band!"

Danni shook her head. "These are my drums, and I need them to make music

sound good everywhere," she said. "They're not meant for one goblin to use selfishly."

Kirsty set him down on the table and he stomped his foot. "Rotten fairy!" he shouted bitterly.

"Now, now," Danni said, "that's not very nice. I think you should get back to Goblin Grotto with your friends before any humans see you. If you promise to go straight there, I'll turn you back to your normal size."

The tiny goblin looked very pouty.

"No way," he said, putting his little hands on his hips.

Danni looked anxiously at Kirsty and Rachel. "We can't leave him running around like this," she said.

Rachel gave her a wink and reached over to stroke the tiny goblin's head. "He's very cute like this," she

said. "Maybe we should keep him
this way."

Kirsty joined in. "Oh yes," she agreed.
"I've got a dollhouse at home. He could
live in that!"

"We can dress him up in some doll
clothes, too," Rachel said, trying not to
giggle. "Wouldn't he look adorable in
a dress?"

The tiny goblin was turning purple with
rage, and his friends were spluttering

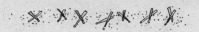

with laughter. "All right, all right," he grumbled. "I'll go home. Just turn me back to normal!"

"OK!" Danni laughed. She waved her wand again, and a swirl of pink sparkles flooded from its tip, streaming all around the miniature goblin. With a faint whooshing sound, he was back to his usual size in an instant. "There," Danni said. "You three can play with the instruments I made up for you, but you must take them back to Goblin Grotto."

The goblins nodded. They knew when they were beaten. "All right," they

muttered sadly. Then they grabbed the
instruments and left.

Danni smiled at
Kirsty and Rachel as
the door closed
behind them.
"Thanks, girls!" she
cried, swooping
down to kiss them
each on the
cheek. "I'm so
happy to have my
drums back again.
It's all thanks to your quick thinking.
Nice work!"

"You're welcome," Kirsty said with a
smile. "That was fun! Did you see the
look on the goblin's face when we
talked about dressing him up in doll

clothes? I thought he was going to explode!"

"I hope he'll think twice before he agrees to any more of Jack Frost's mean schemes," Danni said. "Now, I'd better get back to Fairyland with my magic drums. And you two should get back to the video shoot. I'm sure things will run much more smoothly now that my drums are back safely with me." She winked. "I think they'll find that the instruments are all working perfectly now."

"Thanks, Danni," said Rachel. "I'm really happy we could help. Bye!"

The little fairy vanished in a burst of pretty pink sparkles.

The two girls smiled at one another. "That's four of the magic musical instruments we've helped the fairies find," Kirsty said happily, as they began walking back toward the set. "What a magical, musical vacation this is turning out to be!"

**THE M∪SIC FAIRIES**

Danni the Drum Fairy's magic
instrument is safe and sound in Fairyland!
Can Rachel and Kirsty help

# Maya
## the Harp Fairy?

Join their next adventure in this special
sneak peek. . . .

# Confetti Surprise

"Isn't this a beautiful place for a wedding?" Kirsty Tate said as she and her best friend, Rachel Walker, bounded up the steps of the Wetherbury Hotel. Kirsty was carrying a large package wrapped in sparkly gold paper and tied with a silver bow. Rachel's arms were

full of pink flowers. Both girls were
wearing pretty party dresses.

"Oh, *yes*!" Rachel agreed, glancing up
at the old manor house, its stone walls
covered in rambling ivy. "And the
gardens are gorgeous, too," she added.

The hotel was surrounded by emerald
green lawns and large beds of brightly
colored flowers. There was a tall stone
wall built around the border of the lawns
with elegant archways leading to the rest
of the grounds.

"Isn't it wonderful that Kerry decided
to have her wedding while you're staying
with us for school break, Rachel?" Kirsty
remarked as they paused at the top of the
steps to wait for Mrs. Tate. "I'm so glad
you can come, too!"

Rachel nodded. "It was nice of Kerry to invite us," she replied. "You must have been a *really* good little girl when she was your babysitter, Kirsty!"

Kirsty laughed. "Here's Mom," she said.

Mrs. Tate was hurrying up the steps toward them. "Let's go inside, girls," she said, glancing at her watch. "Kerry's expecting us to be early so we can help finish the decorations for the wedding reception."

The doors to the hotel lobby stood wide open, and Rachel gasped with wonder as they went in. . . .

# RAINBOW magic™

# There's Magic in Every Series!

The Rainbow Fairies

The Weather Fairies

The Jewel Fairies

The Pet Fairies

The Fun Day Fairies

The Petal Fairies

The Dance Fairies

## Read them all!

**█ SCHOLASTIC**

www.scholastic.com

www.rainbowmagiconline.com

HiT entertainment

RMFA

# RAINBOW magic™
## THE PET FAIRIES

# When a pet finds a home, it's magical!

## ■ SCHOLASTIC
www.scholastic.com
www.rainbowmagiconline.com

HiT entertainment

PET

# RAINBOW magic

## These activities are magical!
### Play dress-up, send friendship notes, and much more!

**■SCHOLASTIC**
www.scholastic.com
www.rainbowmagiconline.com

HiT entertainment

RMACTIV2